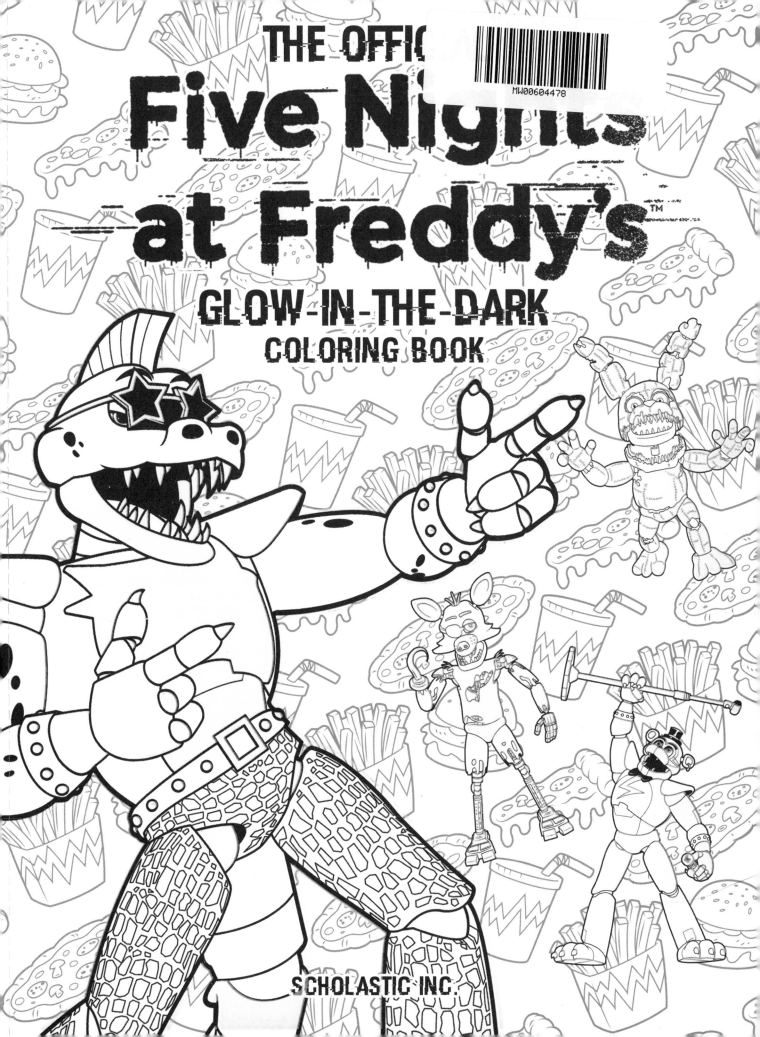

THE OFFIC...
Five Nights
at Freddy's™
GLOW-IN-THE-DARK
COLORING BOOK

SCHOLASTIC INC.

Use your colored pencils or markers to fill in these pages, then make the room dark to see your work glow!

ISBN 978-1-339-04696-9

10 9 8 7 6 5 4 3 2 1   24 25 26 27 28
Printed in China

First printing 2024

Book design by Jeff Shake
Illustrations by Artful Doodlers
Format development, design of glow effects, and book production by Red Bird Publishing UK.

Scholastic UK Ltd., No 1 London Bridge, London SE1 9BG

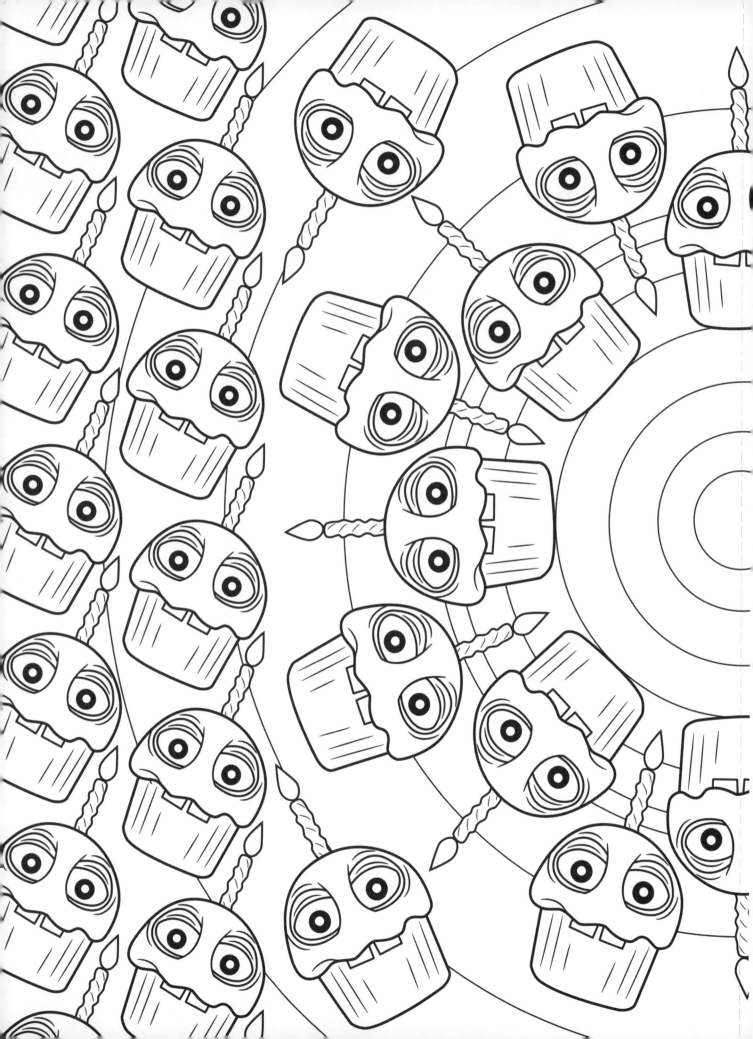

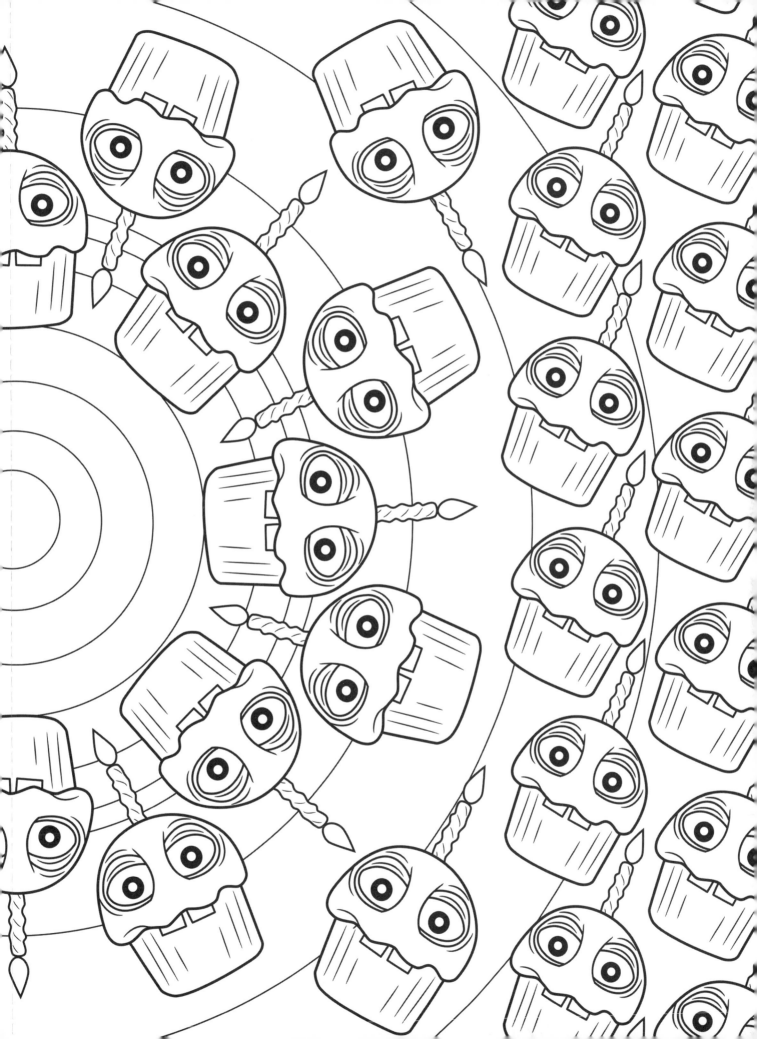

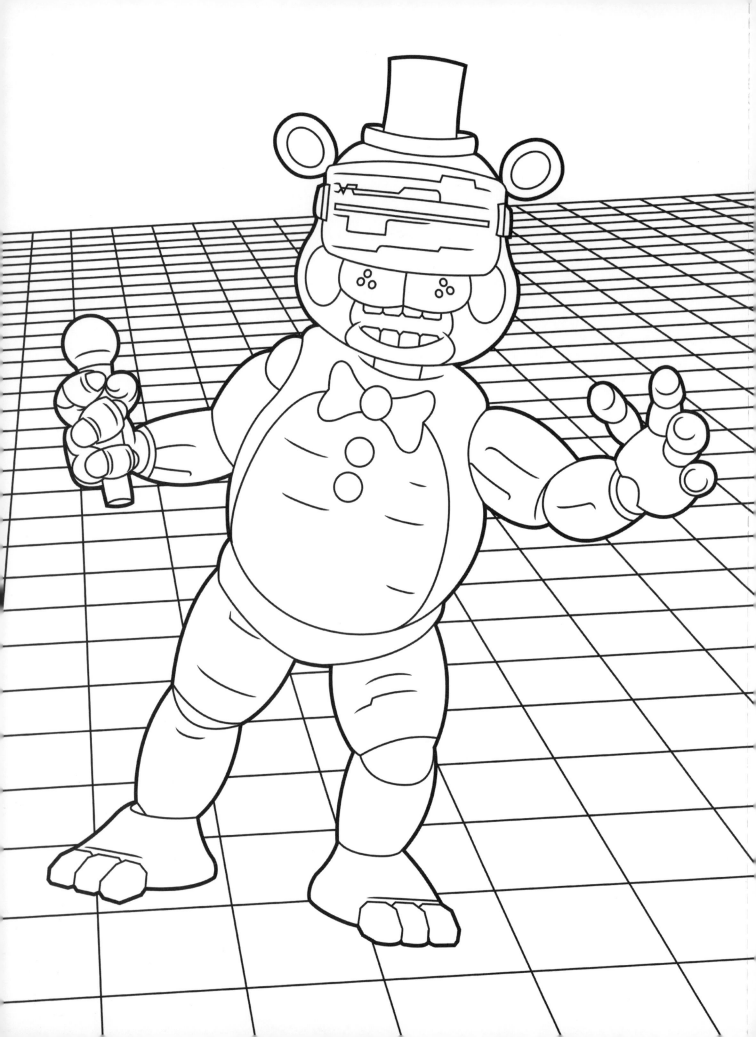

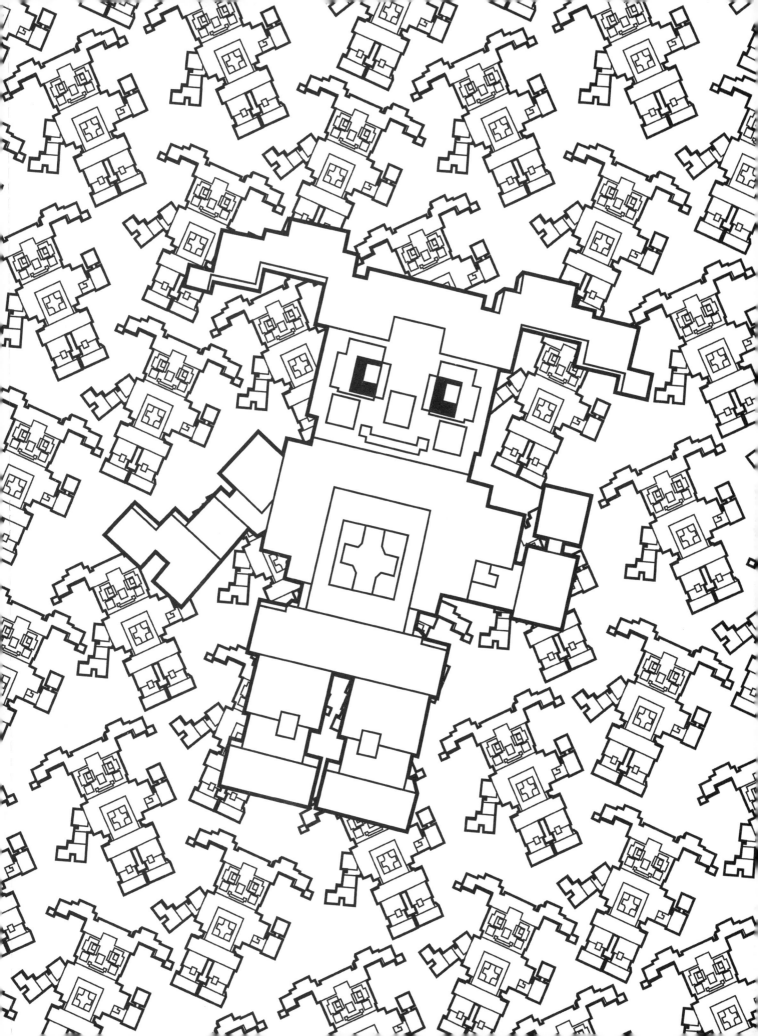